DOGS OF WAR

BY SHEILA KEENAN   ILLUSTRATED BY NATHAN FOX

COLORS BY RICO RENZI AND GUY MAJOR

graphix

An Imprint of

SCHOLASTIC

To all those who have served, sacrificed, and suffered, and to the peacemakers who are trying to put an end to that suffering.

Many thanks to David Saylor for seeing the merits of this book; to Ken Wright for shepherding it through; to Lisa Sandell, an outstanding editor; to Phil Falco, the guy with the design eye; to Jody Corbett and Jennifer Ung for editorial support; and to Rico Renzi and Guy Major for the great color palette.

Major thanks to Nathan Fox for bringing the visual power and glory to these stories!

Above all, thank you, Kevin, for everything.

— S.K.

This book has been a labor of love, an engaging challenge, education, and a flat-out personal joy to be a part of, to say the least. My sincerest thanks to Phil Falco, David Saylor, and Lisa Sandell for making this book possible and their patience, collaboration, and unyielding support throughout it all, and to Sheila Keenan for the opportunity to bring her words, characters, and these great stories to life. And most important, to Jennifer and our daughters — for inspiration, support, and putting up with the late hours, unending talk about dogs, pages to go, and deadlines — all my love. Thank you.

As a young boy, my best friends and pseudo brothers-in-imaginary-arms were a shepherd collie named Stormy and a mutt named Odie. My fondest memories and backyard adventures with them and throughout my youth was with my father. Growing up, he taught me how to respect, train, and care for our dogs, and through the good times and the bad, he and those dogs were always there when I needed them the most. Now, as a father myself with our first puppy (Mr. Truffles), I understand the joy and fun he must have had playing and teaching me those lessons. So to my father and to all of the parents and four-legged best friends out there, and to those whom we have loved and lost, given their lives and service to protect us — I humbly dedicate this book to you. You have and continue to inspire us in more ways than words could ever accomplish — thank you.

— N.F.

Text and compilation copyright © 2013 by Sheila Keenan
Art copyright © 2013 by Nathan Fox

Library of Congress Cataloging-in-Publication Data Available

ISBN 978-0-545-12887-2 (hardcover)
ISBN 978-0-545-12888-9 (paperback)

10 9 8 7 6 5 4 3 2 1   13 14 15 16 17

First edition, November 2013
Lettering by John Green
Book Design by Phil Falco
Edited by Lisa Sandell
Creative Director: David Saylor
Printed in China   38

TABLE OF
CONTENTS

10

OVER HERE, LAD.

HAVE A BIT OF BULLY BEEF.

THANK YOU, SIR.

I'M SERGEANT OLIVER JAMES

MY CORPORAL, WILLIAM CORCORAN.

YOU'VE MET OUR COMPANY JOKERS, JIMMY AND JACK MCMANUS.

TO THE RIGHT THERE IS PRIVATE LIAM O'CONNOR

AND PRIVATE SEAN MURPHY.

AND WHAT WOULD YOUR NAME BE?

MARCELLINUS MCDONALD, SIR. AND THIS IS BOOTS.

MARCELLINUS?

IS THAT A NAME OR A DESSERT?

DUNNO, BUT IT'S TOO LONG FOR THE TRENCHES. BY THE TIME YOU YELL "WATCH YER BACKSIDE, MARCELLINUS," DONNIE HERE WOULD BE A GONER.

HOW OLD ARE YOU, SON?

EIGHTEEN.

HOW OLD ARE YOU?

SIXTEEN, SIR. I'LL BE SEVENTEEN IN THE NEW YEAR.

NEW YEAR? WHO KNOWS IF WE'LL SEE A NEW DAY IN THIS SWAMPY HELL.

DON'T GO ALL GLUM ON US, MURPHY. THREE MORE DAYS AND IT'S CHRISTMAS. THEN WE ROTATE OUT FOR TWO WEEKS. KEEP YOUR HEAD LOW AND WE'LL BE CELEBRATING NEW YEAR'S IN THAT CHARMING VILLAGE BEHIND THE LINES. WE'LL FIND US A NICELY STOCKED PANTRY AND A GOOD, WARM HEARTH.

I'D SETTLE FOR A LONG WALK, COMPLETELY UPRIGHT, NO HIDING BEHIND SANDBAGS AND STOOPING UNDER LOW BEAMS. I JUST WANT TO FEEL THE SUNSHINE ON MY BACK, SEE THE FULL LENGTH OF MY SHADOW.

HE'S A WRITER, THAT ONE.

HEY, LIAM. HOW MANY WORDS ARE THERE FOR MUD?

SO, DONNIE: HOW DID YOU AND BOOTS FALL INTO OUR TRENCH?

THE *HIGHLANDERS*? THEY'RE ENTRENCHED WITH THE BATTALION JUST NORTH OF US. WE HEARD THE GERMANS WALLOPED THEM LAST NIGHT.

I DON'T EXACTLY KNOW, SIR. WE'RE LOST. BOOTS AND I BELONG WITH THE HIGHLANDERS BRIGADE.

BOOTS AND I WERE THERE. EVERYTHING WAS EXPLODING. SO MUCH SMOKE. LOUD, LOUD NOISE. I COULDN'T SEE WHICH WAY TO GO IN THE FOG. I CALLED AND CALLED DR. F.—

WHO'S DR. F.?

I'M HIS ASSISTANT. HE TOOK ME IN; HE GAVE ME BOOTS. HE TREATS ME LIKE A...

I LOST HIM IN THE FLASH. I COULDN'T FIND HIM. *I COULDN'T FIND HIM!*

THERE, THERE, SIP AND DIP, BOY. IT AIN'T THE FRESHEST, BUT YOU NEED IT.

I'VE EATEN WORSE.

AND WHERE WOULD THAT POOR MEAL HAVE BEEN?

IN THE BOYS' HOME.

ARE YOU AN ORPHAN, THEN?

WAS, BUT NOW I HAVE BOOTS AND...

AND THIS DR. F.?

DR. FULHAM CAME TO CHECK OUR THROATS ONE DAY. TOOK A LIKING TO ME AND MADE ME HIS ASSISTANT. I'D CARRY DR. F.'S BAG AND HELP ROUND UP WHATEVER CHICKENS OR EGGS OR PIGLETS FOLKS SOMETIMES PAID HIM WITH.

ONE GENT WAS SO HAPPY WHEN THE DOCTOR HANDED HIM HIS NEWBORN SON, HE OFFERED HIM ONE OF HIS PRIZED COLLIE'S PUPS. DR. FULHAM GAVE ME THE PICK OF THE LITTER.

I CAN'T KEEP A DOG AT THE HOME.

THEN PERHAPS YOU AND THE PUP NEED A NEW HOME. LET'S GO SPEAK TO MRS. FULHAM ABOUT THAT, SHALL WE?

I WENT TO LIVE WITH THE FULHAMS AFTER THAT, UNTIL DR. F. SIGNED ON WITH THE HIGHLANDERS. MRS. FULHAM WAS AS NICE AS THE DOCTOR. I FELT BAD SNEAKING OFF, JUST LEAVING HER A NOTE. BUT WHERE THE DOCTOR GOES, BOOTS AND I GO.

I KNEW DR. FULHAM WOULD NEED ME.

Dear Ma'am,
I've gone to take care of our doctor. Don't worry about me and Boots. This war will be over fast and we'll be home before the lambs drop.
Marcellinus

BOOTS AND I SNUCK INTO THE BAGGAGE CAR WHEN THE HIGHLANDERS WERE LEAVING.

NOBODY NOTICED US.

WHEN THE TRAIN REACHED THE PORT, WELL, THEN I SURPRISED DR. F. HE WASN'T TOO HAPPY AT FIRST, BUT THERE WAS SO MUCH HUBBUB AT THE TIME, WELL, IT WAS JUST EASIER TO TAKE US ALONG.

AFTER THE DOCTOR HEARD ABOUT MERCY DOGS, HE GOT ME AND BOOTS TRAINED FOR SERVICE. AND BOOTS? WELL, SHE'S A HERO.

SHE CAN CRAWL ON OUT THROUGH NO-MAN'S-LAND AND NO MAN'LL SEE OR HEAR HER. SHE HUNKERS DOWN LOW AND QUIET AND SNIFFS AROUND IN THE DARK, LOOKING FOR POOR FELLOWS THAT ARE SHOT UP.

THEN SHE COMES BACK, WE GET OUR STRETCHERS, AND BOOTS LEADS US TO THE LIVE ONES.

THERE'S MORE THAN ONE BLOKE WHO'D HAVE BEEN LEFT FOR DEAD, UNSEEN IN THE MUCK OR BRUSH, IF IT WEREN'T FOR MY DOG.

WELL, LAD, THAT'S A GOOD STORY, WHICH WE ALL HOPE HAS A HAPPY ENDING. I'LL SEND WORD OUT TO YOUR REGIMENT THAT YOU'RE HERE AND SEE WHAT WE CAN FIND OUT ABOUT YOUR DOCTOR.

RIGHT, GIRL. YOU'RE A GOOD DOG, YOU ARE. BEST FRIEND I EVER HAD.

LET'S HOPE YOU AND DR. FULHAM ARE SOON BACK HOME CURING PEOPLE, AND WE SOON STOP KILLING THEM.

TO GOING HOME!

IN ONE PIECE... OR AT LEAST WITH ONLY A LITTLE WOUND, A SMALL, HEROIC *BLIGHTY*, NOTHING TOO BLOODY.

JUST ENOUGH OF A SCRATCH TO GET ME HOME...

AND MAYBE A MEDAL OR TWO.

WELL, NOBODY'S GOING HOME TODAY, GENTS, AND WE'VE GOT HOUSEKEEPING TO DO HERE. THIS BLOODY RAIN IS TURNING OUR TRENCHES INTO CANALS. WE'RE ON THE PUMP SHIFT. DONNIE, YOU'LL WORK ALONGSIDE ME.

AND THEN WHAT? AFTER MRS. F. HAS CRIED AND FUSSED OVER YOU AND STUFFED YOU FULL OF HER BEST LAMB STEW, THEN WHAT, MY BOY?

I'M THINKING I'LL TALK TO DR. FULHAM ABOUT GOING TO SCHOOL. MAYBE BECOME A VETERINARIAN.

I LIKE ANIMALS. YOU CAN DEPEND ON THEM.

LOOK...

POOR LAD.

PRIVATE MURPHY, THAT KIND OF TALK WILL NOT HELP THE WAR EFFORT....

FODDER, WE'RE JUST FODDER. THIS WAS ALL SUPPOSED TO BE OVER IN NO TIME. WHAT HAPPENED TO OUR QUICK VICTORY?

THE ONLY WAY TO WIN THIS WAR IS TO RUN OUT OF BULLETS... OR *BODIES*.

BOTH OF YOU: PUT A SOCK IN IT AND LET'S GET THIS SOLDIER PROPERLY BURIED. ANY IDENTIFICATION TAGS ON HIM?

THE NEXT DAY AND

THE NEXT DAY AND

THE NEXT . . .

COME ON, GIRL, LET'S TAKE A WALK. I CAN'T BE COOPED UP ANYMORE. . . .

GERMANS OR NO GERMANS.

-TOK-

BOOTS, CATCH!

KLATCH!

WHAT IS IT, GIRL?

NIGHTFALL.

THE GERMANS STARTED SHELLING.

AND DIDN'T STOP.

YOU'RE A GOOD DOG, BOOTS. WHAT WOULD I DO HERE WITHOUT YOU, EH?

WE'RE A PAIR ALL RIGHT, GOT TO STICK TOGETHER.

WHAT ARE YOU WRITING?

MEMORIES. THINGS I REMEMBER.

LIKE WHAT?

LIKE THE PRECISE WAY MY FIANCÉE PRESSES HER THUMB ALL THE WAY AROUND THE DOUGH OF AN APPLE PIE WHEN SHE'S BAKING, SO THE CRUST IS A CIRCLE OF PERFECT HALF-MOONS.

THAT'S A STRANGE KIND OF THING TO THINK ABOUT IN THIS PLACE.

THAT'S EXACTLY WHY I'M THINKING ABOUT IT—IT'S *NOT* THIS PLACE. IT'S NOT BULLETS AND BLOOD AND MUD. IT'S NOT MEN LITERALLY SINKING TO THEIR LOWEST DEPTHS.

I'M TRYING TO REMEMBER WHAT'S GOOD AND BEAUTIFUL IN THIS WORLD, WHAT WOULD YOU SAY?

I DUNNO.

BOOTS IS BEAUTIFUL.

THAT'S IT. I'M OUT.

PASS ME A BIT OF BARKER ON YOUR WAY—AND I WANT A PIECE THE RATS HAVEN'T CHEWED ON FIRST.

WHAT'S THE MATTER? NEVER BEEN ON A COOTIE SAFARI? BRING YOURSELF AND THAT WALKING FLEA HOTEL OVER HERE AND JOIN IN.

SANTA CLAUS IS HERE!

PLUM PUDDING? WHAT WOULD CHRISTMAS BE WITHOUT IT?

DELICIOUS.

AHH! BUTTERSCOTCH.

JUST IN TIME. THE RATS HAVE EATEN THROUGH THE OTHER MILLION POUNDS OF STUFF THAT THE GOOD WOMEN OF BRITAIN HAVE SENT US.

INGRATE. WHERE'S YOUR CHRISTMAS CHEER?

AT HOME, WHERE MY STOCKING IS HUNG.

LOOKS LIKE HER ROYAL HIGHNESS IS THINKING OF US.

THE NEXT DAY, CHRISTMAS

ENGLANDER!

ENGLANDER!

WHAT'S OUR ENEMY FRITZ UP TO?

WHAT DO YOU SEE, OLLIE?

LADS, I BELIEVE THEY'RE RAISING A PINT TO US.

DON'T TRUST THOSE HUNS, IT'S A TRICK.

MAYBE THEY MEAN WHAT THEY SAY. IT'S *CHRISTMAS*.

ENGLANDER, COME OUT! YOU NO SHOOT, WE NO SHOOT.

NO, NOBODY GO. NO!

A CHRISTMAS TOAST AND A CHAT *WOULD* BE NICE, WOULDN'T IT?

YOU'RE CRAZY.

BUT WHAT IF THE GERMANS MEAN IT? MAYBE THEY'RE TIRED OF FIGHTING, TOO.

39

WE'VE GOT LEAVE TO BURY OUR DEAD. THE GERMANS WILL BE OUT DOING THE SAME. CORKIE, GET OUR SHOVELS. MURPHY, YOU STAY ON WATCH HERE.

WHAT ABOUT ME, SIR?

NO-MAN'S-LAND ISN'T FOR YOU, DONNIE. KEEP YOUR YOUTH.

I CAN HOLD MY OWN, AND I WANT TO DO MY SHARE. YOU THINK I HAVEN'T SEEN DEAD PEOPLE?

SNIFF SNIFF

NOT LIKE THIS. IT'S NOT RIGHT, NO ONE SHOULD SEE THE DEAD, NO ONE SHOULD *BE* DEAD LIKE THIS.

TAK!

I'M THE ONE WHO'S A DOCTOR'S ASSISTANT.

SIGH!
ALL RIGHT, ALL RIGHT, THEN. YOU FOLLOW BEHIND US. WE'LL SIGNAL IF THE MAN'S IN ONE PIECE. THEN YOU CAN LOOK FOR PERSONAL EFFECTS WE CAN SEND ON HOME TO HIS LOVED ONES.

I JUST DON'T THINK A MACHINE GUN IS SPORTING . . . NOT A *REAL* SOLDIER'S KIND OF WEAPON, KNOW WHAT I MEAN? NO SKILL INVOLVED.

HOW ABOUT WE PLAY FOR THAT POT YOU GOT ON YOUR HEAD?

MEIN PICKELHAUBE? AND FROM YOU?

A GENUINE BRASS TIN FROM THE ROYAL PRINCESS HERSELF. LOVELY LITTLE SOUVENIR FOR YOUR MISSUS OR SWEETHEART.

HA HA HA!

JA. IN SCHOOL, WE LEARN IT. AND MY BROTHER TEACHES ME. HE GOES TO MANCHESTER TO WORK . . . UNTIL ALL THIS. YOU WOULD LIKE SOME CHOCOLATE?

THANKS.

YOUR DOG IS WET, MUDDY. WE SHOULD MAKE A FIRE.

45

47

WELL, FRITZ, I WON THIS FAIR AND SQUARE, BUT—

MERRY CHRISTMAS. HERE YOU GO, MATE.

♪ AULD LANG SYNE ♫

YES, YES. AFTER THIS IS ALL OVER, I WOULD VERY MUCH LIKE TO SEE YOUR CITY.

AND I WILL SEE THESE LETTERS GET MAILED TO YOUR FATHER-IN-LAW IN LONDON.

AUF WIEDERSEHEN, BOOTS, GOOD-BYE.

AUF WIEDERSEHEN, MY FRIEND.

GOOD-BYE.

WORD DOWN THE LINE IS THAT THE BRASS HATS BACK AT HEADQUARTERS WEREN'T TOO HAPPY ABOUT OUR FRATERNIZING LAST NIGHT.

FRATERNIZING, THAT'S A BIG WORD, CORKIE. I THOUGHT IT WAS JUST AT A LITTLE CARD GAME.

FRATERNIZING WITH THE ENEMY IS A COURT-MARTIAL OFFENSE. LET'S HOPE HEADQUARTERS HAS MORE PRESSING MATTERS TO WORRY ABOUT.

SEEMS THAT THEY DO. I JUST GOT ORDERS THAT WE'RE INVITED TO A WIRING PARTY TONIGHT.

I'M BUSY.

I'M AFRAID OF THE DARK!

THERE ARE RUMORS THE GERMANS PLAN TO BRING IN FRESH ARTILLERY. OUR ORDERS ARE TO CHECK AND REPAIR OUR BARBED WIRE FENCES AND STRING SOME NEW WIRE AT THE SOUTH END BEFORE THEY DO.

BUT WE'RE ROTATING OUT TOMORROW, AREN'T WE?

YES, LADDIES, IT'S OUR TURN TO GO OUT FOR A REST, BUT THAT'S TOMORROW AND THERE'S STILL TONIGHT IN BETWEEN. ORDERS ARE ORDERS.

MURPHY, YOU'LL STAY HERE ON GUARD.

AND, BOOTS, YOU JUST STAY.

DONNIE, YOU STAY AWAKE WITH HIM.

SHOOT! SHOOT! KILL THAT SNIPER!

TOO LOUD! MAKE IT STOP! MAKE IT STOP!

58

THE END

EARLY SPRING, 1942

SONDRESTROM AIR BASE, CODE NAME: BLUIE WEST 8
KANGERLUSSUAQ, GREENLAND
35 MILES NORTH OF THE ARCTIC CIRCLE

THE JAPANESE BOMBED PEARL HARBOR ON DECEMBER 7, 1941, AND PRESIDENT FRANKLIN ROOSEVELT DECLARED WAR THE NEXT DAY. . . .

BUT IN GREENLAND, CODE NAME "BLUIE,"

THE U.S. ARMY AIR FORCE HAD ALREADY BEEN AT WAR FOR SIX MONTHS,

SECRETLY BUILDING MILITARY AIRSTRIPS AND WEATHER STATIONS IN RECORD TIME.

WELCOME TO BLUIE WEST 8.

BUT AFTER PEARL HARBOR, WE'RE NOT GOING TO LET THAT HAPPEN, RIGHT, BOYS? NO SURPRISES ON *THIS* COAST.

NOW, STOW YOUR GEAR, GET SOME CHOW, REST UP, AND BE READY AT 0700 HOURS TOMORROW.

WHICH ONE OF YOU IS COOPER?

I AM, SARGE.

HMPHF. FIGURES. SAYS HERE YOU'RE A DOG MAN.

UHHH, RIGHT. CAME THROUGH TRAINING AT PRESQUE ISLE, BUT I'M A MAINE MAN; BEEN DOGSLEDDING ALL MY LIFE. I CAN HANDLE A TEAM.

WE'LL SEE ABOUT THAT. BE READY TOMORROW AT 0700 SHARP TO MEET THE DOGS.

WHO DIDN'T PLUG THE BLASTED KEYHOLE? COOPER! GET OVER HERE AND BRING A SHOVEL! WE GOT DOGS TO SEE TO.

THAT'S WHAT A 100-MILE-PER-HOUR WIND WILL DO IN NO TIME. *SHOVEL!*

SHUFF SHUFF SHLUFF

BRAM

GOOD MORNING, GREENLAND!

HAROOOOOOO

POFF! POFF

AAAAOOOOOO!

HOWLOOOOO HOWLOOOOOO HOWLOOOOO

COOPER! THEY'RE A DOG TEAM, NOT A CHOIR! FEED 'EM SO THEY SHUT UP.

HERE YOU GO, PUPS, SOME NICE DRIED FISH AND SOME DELICIOUS WALRUS SKIN FOR DESSERT.

DOESN'T THAT WALRUS FAT TASTE GOOD?

HERE, BOY.

WATCH OUT FOR LOKI, HE'S A TRICKY ONE. HE'LL DO ANYTHING FOR FOOD AND THAT'S ABOUT IT. HARD TO GET HIM TO DO WHAT YOU WANT IN THE HARNESS.

I'D SHIP HIM BACK STATESIDE IF I WASN'T ALREADY SHORT A DOG.

STAY, LOKI.

HE'S A STRONG-LOOKING DOG, SARGE. MAYBE I CAN WORK WITH HIM.

SUIT YOURSELF. FINISH UP HERE AND GET OVER TO THE MESS IF YOU WANT BREAKFAST WHILE IT'S HOT.

BAD DOG, NO!

BUT YOU'RE A GOOD DOG, RIGHT, LOKI? OR AT LEAST YOU COULD BE. SEE YOU LATER, BOY.

73

DOGS ALL SET?

ALL SET.

GOOD.

YOU BEEN HERE LONG, SARGE?

SHIPPED IN WITH THE FIRST CREW AND DOG TEAM, BACK IN THE FALL. WE ATE AND SLEPT IN TENTS. BUILT ALL THIS, RIGHT DOWN TO THE AIRFIELD, IN SIX MONTHS.

THAT MUST HAVE BEEN ROUGH.

ROUGH? IT WAS DOWNRIGHT *PRIMITIVE* UNTIL WE BUILT THOSE SHACKS WE NOW CALL HOME. DIDN'T BOTHER BIG DAVE, THOUGH, RIGHT, SARGE?

YEAH, EXCEPT FOR THAT ONE NIGHT...

THERE WAS THIS ONE BUCK PRIVATE, ALWAYS GRIPING, DROVE EVERYBODY CRAZY. KEPT NATTERING AWAY, EVEN WHEN WE FINALLY HAD FOUR WALLS AND A ROOF AROUND US. ONE WINDY NIGHT, HE WENT ON AND ON ABOUT HAVING TO WEAR THE SAME SMELLY LONG JOHNS DAY IN, DAY OUT. FINALLY, BIG DAVE WALKED OVER, GRABBED THAT BUCK'S UNION SUIT, AND STUFFED IT UP THE FLUE. SHOT RIGHT UP.

THE NEXT DAY

LOKI! HAW, OVER!

HUK-HUK!

AI-AI!

STOP.

HUK-HUK!

GEE! GEE! GEE!

THIS IS GOING TO TAKE SOME WORK.

YOU DON'T KNOW LEFT FROM RIGHT, LOKI!

GEE! GEE! GEE!

HAW! HAW! HAW!

OKAY, BOY. WE'RE GOING TO BE DOING THIS EVERY DAY. SO START PAYING ATTENTION.

LOKI, WHOA!

LOKI, GEE!

SEE, SARGE, HE'S A FAST LEARNER!

LATER THAT DAY

COOPER! GET THAT MUTT OUT OF HERE! ALL HE'S LEARNED IS WHERE SPAM COMES FROM!

LOKI! STAY!

DROP IT!

COME TO ME!

HE JUST NEEDS A LITTLE MORE WORK, SARGE. I CAN DO IT.

ONE MORE CHANCE, OR ELSE I'M SELLING HIM OFF TO A GREENLANDER.

AND I TOLD YOU: NO TREATS!

THE NEXT FEW WEEKS

GEE! HAW!

HUK-HUK!

HOOKWA-HOOKWA!

RUN, BOY, GOOD DOG!

GOOD BOY, LOKI!

PAK BAK PLAFF

LATER THAT MONTH

CUT IT OUT, BOY, THAT TICKLES.

YOU NEED A PEDICURE. YOU DON'T WANT ICE BALLS GUMMING UP YOUR PADS, DO YOU? AND THESE NAILS ARE TOO LONG. THEY'LL HURT YOUR TOES WHEN YOU'RE PULLING THE SLED.

STAY, LOKI.

HEY, SARGE, WHAT DO I HAVE TO DO TODAY? POLISH ALL THE DOG BOWLS?

I JUST GOT WORD FROM A DANISH TRAWLER. SAID THEY WERE BOARDED AND THEN FORCED TO LAND SOME GERMANS NOT TOO FAR UP FROM HERE. COULD BE RECONNAISSANCE.

I'M TAKING A SLED UP ON THE RIDGE TO SEE WHAT I CAN SEE.

VOLUNTEERING FOR SERVICE.

I CAN HELP, SARGE. I'VE BEEN WORKING THESE DOGS FOR WEEKS.

HARNESS THE DOGS AND BRING YOUR GUN.

WEATHER LOOKS CHANGEABLE. BETTER BE PREPARED FOR ANYTHING.

TUG TUG

CRNCH CRNCH

AIN'T YOU THE CAT'S MEOW.

WOULD'VE BEEN ONE *BIG* CAT WHO SPORTED THAT FUR.

THEY'RE *NANUS*, YOU KNUCKLEHEADS, POLAR BEAR PANTS. PAID A LOCAL GUY, A HUNTER, FOR THEM. THESE PANTS'LL KEEP ME WARM FOR FIVE YEARS.

THIS WAR AIN'T GONNA LAST FIVE YEARS. NOT WITH US IN IT.

AI—AI!

KRSHH

I DON'T LIKE THE WAY THIS SKY LOOKS, COULD SNOW.

LET'S DO THE HANSEL AND GRETEL AND STICK A COUPLE OF THESE IN TO SHOW THE WAY HOME, JUST IN CASE.

SHUNK

VWRRRRR

THAT SLED'S FLYING IN THE MILK.

IS IT OURS? OR IS IT . . . THE NAZIS?

NO TELLING FROM HERE, BUT WHOEVER IT IS CAN'T SEE US, EITHER. IN THIS OVERCAST, THEY COULDN'T EVEN SEE A HORIZON. A PILOT MAY LOSE ALL REFERENCE POINTS.

LET'S KEEP GOING WHILE WE'RE STILL HIDDEN. IF WE CAN GET UP ON THE RIDGE, WE'LL HAVE A CLEARER VIEW OF THE COASTS. MAYBE WE'LL SPOT THOSE NAZIS.

VWRROOOOOOOOOO

RRROOOOOOOMM

ILLI, ILLI, ILLI!

CRAK CRAK

SECURE
THE SLED.
WE'LL SKI IN
CLOSER.

GR

STAY, BOY.
STAY.

IT'S A P-38, ONE OF OURS. HEY IN THERE, CAN YOU HEAR ME?

HELLOOOO!

DOESN'T LOOK GOOD FROM OVER HERE.

LET'S CIRCLE ALL THE WAY AROUND AND CHECK.

CHECK FOR ANY WHITE DOTS, MAKE SURE HE'S NOT FROSTBITTEN. THEN PUT VASELINE ALL OVER HIS FACE SO HIS SKIN DOESN'T FREEZE.

CHECK.

WE'LL BOTH SKI ALONG, LIGHTEN THE LOAD ON THE DOGS. READY?

READY.

CRAK!

WHOA, CAESAR! AI-AI!

SARGE! WATCH OUT!

COOPER! STOP THE DOGS!

WHOA, WHOA, WHOA.

NORDEN . . . NORDEN . . .

COOPER, HELP ME HERE. LET'S GET THIS PILOT BACK ON THAT SLED.

NORDEN. IT'S A PRECISION BOMBSIGHT. TOP SECRET WEAPON. JUST A FEW OF US HERE IN THE KNOW. WITH THAT SUCKER, A BOMB CAN DROP ITS PAYLOAD INTO A PICKLE BARREL FROM 20,000 FEET UP. IF A PLANE GOES DOWN WITH A NORDEN, THE PILOT IS SUPPOSED TO SHOOT IT. MAKE SURE THE ENEMY DOESN'T GET HOLD OF IT. SOUNDS LIKE THIS GUY DIDN'T GET THE CHANCE TO PULL THE TRIGGER.

I'M GOING BACK TO THE CRASH.

BUT YOUR BOOTS . . . YOU NEED TO GET YOUR FEET WARM AND DRY OR YOU'LL BE FROSTBITTEN IN NO TIME, MAYBE EVEN LOSE YOUR TOES. I CAN GO.

BUT YOU'VE NEVER BEEN OUT ON YOUR OWN, AND THAT NAZI REPORT—

WE'VE BEEN LOOKING FOR HOURS AND HAVEN'T SEEN HIDE NOR HAIR OF THEM.

THE PLANE'S NOT THAT FAR BACK. I CAN SKI THERE IN NO TIME, THEN CATCH UP WITH YOU. YOU'LL BE MOVING SLOWER WITH TWO MEN ON BOARD ANYHOW.

BUT . . .

MOAN . . .

I'M GOOD, SARGE, I CAN DO IT. YOU'VE GOT TO GET HIM BACK FAST.

YOU'LL NEED A FEW THINGS.

KEEP YOUR WEAPON OUT SO IT STAYS FROZEN, OTHERWISE MOISTURE CONDENSES, AND WHEN YOU PULL IT OUT, IT JAMS WITH ICE. KNOW HOW TO BUILD A SNOW WALL IF YOU NEED TO?

I'M FROM MAINE, REMEMBER? I SNOW-CAMPED AS A BOY.

HERE, TAKE SOME GOLDFISH AND LET'S SPLIT THE WATER.

WHEN YOU GET TO THE PLANE, HEAD RIGHT FOR THE BOMBER'S SEAT, SHOOT THAT NORDEN UP GOOD, AND GET OUT OF THERE.

DON'T BE A HERO, THIS ISN'T A MOVIE. IN. OUT. AND KEEP YOUR EYES PEELED ALONG THE WAY BACK. SHOOT ANYTHING THAT MOVES.

GOT IT, SARGE. I'M READY.

TAKE THIS, TOO. THEY SAY IT BRINGS LUCK, MAKES YOU STRONG LIKE *NANOQ*.

I EXPECT YOU TO BRING IT BACK, SOLDIER!

SURE THING, SARGE.

NOW GET GOING . . . AND HURRY.

97

BLASTED DOG! YOU'VE SPOILED HIM. HE'LL UPSET THE TEAM.

CAN THE TEAM PULL WITHOUT HIM, SARGE?

NOW IT CAN.

TAKE THAT MUTT WITH YOU.

HUK!

HUK!

LOKI, AI-AI!

SHFF

NOTHING, BOY. MUST BE SPOOKING MYSELF.

LET'S GO, LOKI.

STEADY, BOY.
STAY.

COME,
LOKI.

GOOD DOG. WE DID IT . . . .

SURPRISE, THAT'S THE ONLY WAY. BUT HOW CAN WE SURPRISE 'EM . . .

. . . IF I DON'T KNOW WHERE THEY ARE?

THOSE DIDN'T HELP YOU MUCH ANYHOW, DID THEY? NEVER SAW US COMING.

JUST A MANNER OF SPEAKING, LOKI.

CRUNCH

THERE WERE ONLY THREE, ONLY THREE....

LATER, BACK AT THE BASE

THE PRISONERS ARE SECURED.

YOU GET THE THIRD GUY?

THE ONE YOU CONKED? HUEY, DEWEY, AND LOUIE HERE BROUGHT HIM TO THEIR SLED.

AND OUR PILOT?

HE'S GONNA MAKE IT.

HOW'D YOU FIND ME, ANYWAY?

WHEN YOU DIDN'T CATCH UP WITH ME, I KNEW THERE WAS TROUBLE.... ME AND THE BOYS SKIED BACK TO THE PLANE—

—OR WHAT WAS LEFT OF IT.

WE THOUGHT YOU AND THE POOCH WERE GONERS, DOWN THE HOLE.

BUT THEN SARGE SPOTTED FOOTPRINTS . . .

... PAWPRINTS ...

... AND SKI TRACKS ...

CUT TO THE CHASE!

THE NAZIS WERE ON YOUR TAIL, SO WE GOT ON THEIRS.

THANKS, FELLAS. I WAS LOOKING FOR A RIDE HOME. I OWE YOU.

YOU SURE DO OWE ME SOMETHING. . . .

BUT I OWE YOU EVEN MORE, BOY.

THE END

YESTERDAY

TODAY

TOMORROW

...AND THEN IT WAS.

LIFE IS GOOD WITH A DOG.

ESPECIALLY 'CAUSE THERE ISN'T MUCH LIFE AROUND HERE. MOST PEOPLE GO TO WORK. I'M THE ONLY ONE UNDER A HUNDRED WHO'S HOME ALL DAY.

MAMA SAYS I'LL FEEL BETTER IN SEPTEMBER. YOU KNOW IT'S BAD WHEN SCHOOL LOOKS GOOD.

BOY, GET THAT HOUND AWAY FROM ME! RUDENESS!

THAT'S OUR NEIGHBOR MRS. JOHNSON. SHE THINKS SHE'S SO FINE BECAUSE SHE'S THE ONLY ONE AROUND HERE WITH A WORKING TV. SHE'S GOT IT TURNED ON ALL THE TIME, JUST TO REMIND US.

SORRY, MRS. JOHNSON, HERE, BOUNCER.

THE TRAILER NEXT TO US IS EMPTY . . . OR SO I THOUGHT.

BOUNCER, STOP THAT! DOWN, BOY!

SPLAT!

THAT'S IT! GET RID OF THAT MUTT! NO DOGS!

PLEASE, MR. TIBBETS, I'M SORRY. HE'S JUST A PUPPY, HE WON'T DO IT AGAIN.

I SAID, GET RID OF HIM... OR I WILL!

THE BOY'S GONNA CLEAN ALL THIS UP.

I'M NOT GOING TO STAND FOR...

BOY, START PICKING UP THAT TRASH.

CRAZY VET!

HADO!

LOOK AT YOU. WHO MADE YOU A SOUL MAN?

YOU KNOW YOU DID, L.

BUMMP

CAN'T BELIEVE IT, MAN. I THOUGHT BOOT CAMP WAS IT—GOOD TIMES, THEN GOOD-BYE, NEVER SEE YOU AGAIN, BROTHER.

AND WHAT'S THAT?

NOT *WHAT*, HADO, *WHO*.

THIS IS THE QUEEN OF DOGS, SHEBA, SAY HELLO TO THE SORRIEST SON EVER DRAFTED.

BARK

GOOD GIRL! GIVE ME SOME LOVE.

I HAD TO KEEP BOUNCER AWAY FROM TROUBLE WITH A *T*, AS IN TIBBETS. AFTER MAMA WENT TO WORK, WE HEADED OUT BEHIND THE TRAILER PARK TO PLAY.

THERE'S A NICE BIG FIELD BACK THERE, PROBABLY SOMEBODY'S FARM ONCE.

NOBODY BOTHERED ME AND BOUNCER OUT THERE. WE HUNTED FOR OLD STUFF.

OR EXPLORED THE BROKEN-DOWN SHACK. OR JUST RAN AROUND LIKE CRAZY THINGS.

ONCE, BOUNCER TOOK OFF AFTER A SQUIRREL OR SOMETHING. AND RAN ME RAGGED TRYING TO GET HIM BACK.

PLASH!

SOMETIMES I FELT LIKE WE WERE BEING WATCHED.

BUT I DIDN'T LOOK BACK. IF PEOPLE WANTED TO PLAY INVISIBLE MAN, IT'S NO BUSINESS OF MINE.

BUT I SAW THINGS . . .

AND I HEARD THINGS . . .

YOU KNOW MUCH ABOUT THAT VIETNAM GUY NEXT DOOR, THAT VET?

I HEAR SOME OF THEM COME BACK A LITTLE . . . YOU KNOW . . .

HE ANY TROUBLE?

I'LL TELL YOU WHAT'S TROUBLE. THE BOTTOM OF MY SINK WHAT'S RUSTING OUT, **THAT'S** TROUBLE. YOU WANNA COME SEE ABOUT **THAT?**

UH, YEAH, FIRST THING . . . TOMORROW.

BOUNCER!

WOW, YOU DREW ALL THESE? ARE YOU AN ARTIST?

IS THIS VIETNAM?

YEAH, I DREW THEM. IT DON'T MEAN NOTHING.

THAT'S 'NAM.

I READ ABOUT THE VIETNAM WAR. MAMA AND I WERE JUST TALKING ABOUT IT.

WHAT'S YOUR MAMA KNOW ABOUT 'NAM? WHAT'S ANYBODY BACK IN THE WORLD HERE KNOW ABOUT THE WAR?

WELL, WHY DON'T YOU TELL ME ABOUT IT, THEN?

WHAT GOOD IS TELLING YOU? WHAT GOOD IS TELLING ANYONE?

I WAS JUST ASKING.

WHO DO YOU THINK YOU ARE? YOU THINK YOU AND YOUR POOCH AND YOUR MAMA'S PIE MAKE EVERYTHING ALL OKAY?

IS THAT WHAT YOU THINK?

I DON'T THINK ANYTHING. I'M JUST NOBODY WHO KNOWS NOTHING. JUST THE DUMB KID NEXT DOOR WITH HIS BAD DOG.

YOU EVER LIVE EVERY DAY WONDERING IF YOU WERE GONNA BE KILLED BY PEOPLE YOU CAN'T SEE? BUT YOU KNOW THEY'RE OUT THERE, MAD CRAZY TO KILL YOU.

THEN YOU COME HOME AND MORE MAD CRAZIES ARE CALLING *YOU* THE KILLER? YOU EVER BEEN *SPIT* ON?

YEAH.

PLASH!

COME ON, BOUNCER, LET'S GO.

HENRY, I'M . . .

I GOT TWO COKES . . . YOU WANT ONE?

WHEN LANFORD WENT TO GET THE SODAS, I INCHED A LITTLE CLOSER TO THE PICTURES TO GET A BETTER LOOK. SOME OF THEM WERE SMUDGED, LIKE THEY'D GOTTEN WET. SOME WERE STAINED.

I HOPE THAT ISN'T BLOOD.

IT'S TABASCO SAUCE . . . IN CASE YOU'RE WONDERING.

THAT'S MY GOOD BUDDY HADO. HE ALWAYS TRAVELED WITH A BOTTLE OF IT. WHATEVER GLOP WAS IN THAT C RATION, HE JUST POURED THE HOT SAUCE ON LIKE KETCHUP. SWORE IT CUT THROUGH THE GREASE. GOOD FOR KILLING OFF LEECHES, TOO.

LEECHES?

TAK!

BIG SUCKERS. IF IT CRAWLS, FLIES, BITES, AND MAKES YOU SUFFER, IT LIVES IN 'NAM.

I HAD TO GROOM SHEBA REAL GOOD TO CHECK FOR BITES AND MAKE SURE NOTHING STUCK TO HER.

IS THIS SHEBA?

ARMY RULES: DOGS ARE EQUIPMENT, LIKE YOUR GUN OR YOUR AMMO; YOU GOT TO LEAVE IT ALL BEHIND AND WALK AWAY WHEN YOUR TIME'S UP.

LANFORD WENT ALL QUIET ON ME AGAIN. I DIDN'T WANT TO GET KICKED OUT OF HIS TRAILER, BECAUSE I WASN'T FINISHED LOOKING AT THE PICTURES YET. AND IT'S NOT LIKE I HAD ANYWHERE ELSE INTERESTING TO GO. I HAD TO COME UP WITH SOMETHING TO SAY, FAST.

I'LL BET SHEBA WAS A GOOD DOG.

THE BEST.

WHAT'S A DOG DO IN VIETNAM, ANYHOW?

SAVE LIVES, THAT'S WHAT A SCOUT DOG DOES.

SHEBA COULD SENSE EVERY SNIPER . . .

. . . BOOBY TRAP . . .

. . . AND DAISY CHAIN

THAT WAS LYING IN WAIT FOR THE BOYS.

SHEBA COULD *HEAR* THE WIND VIBRATING TRIP WIRES.

THAT NIGHT I DID SOME HARD THINKING.

I WAS BEGINNING TO SEE WHY LANFORD DIDN'T WANT TO TALK ABOUT VIETNAM. THIS WAR BUSINESS WAS SO COMPLICATED. ME AND MY OLD FRIENDS USED TO PLAY WAR AND PRETEND-SHOOT EACH OTHER IN THE WOODS FOR HOURS. I TRIED TO IMAGINE WHAT IT WOULD BE LIKE IF ONE OF US NEVER GOT BACK UP.

I THOUGHT ABOUT LANFORD AND SHEBA AND ALL THE FRIENDLY LOOKING GUYS HE DREW. NONE OF THOSE PICTURES LOOKED LIKE THE WAR ON THE NEWS. MAYBE I OUGHTA STOP WORRYING ABOUT WHAT LANFORD DID IN VIETNAM. I DIDN'T RIGHTFULLY KNOW, DID I? AND WHAT ARE YOU *SUPPOSED* TO DO WHEN SOMEBODY'S SHOOTING AT YOU?

ONE OF MAMA'S FAVORITE SAYINGS ABOUT FOLKS POPPED INTO MY HEAD. *WALK A MILE IN HIS SHOES*, SHE'D SAY IF I WAS GETTING ALL RILED UP ABOUT SOMEBODY.

BUT I *COULDN'T* WALK A MILE IN LANFORD'S SHOES. THOSE ARMY BOOTS WERE TOO BIG FOR ME.

COME ON, BOUNCER. BE A GOOD DOG AND LIE DOWN.

I DECIDED TO STICK TO THE FACTS: THIS DOG NEEDED SOME TRAINING!

HEY, LANFORD.

HEY.

I WAS THINKING MAYBE IF YOU WEREN'T TOO BUSY, WELL . . . MAYBE YOU COULD SHOW ME HOW YOU TRAINED SHEBA. I MEAN WITH BOUNCER.

YOU DON'T WANT YOUR DOG GOING INTO NO WAR.

MR. TIBBETS IS GONNA GO TO WAR *ON ME* IF BOUNCER GETS INTO ANY MORE TROUBLE. COULDN'T YOU JUST HELP ME OUT WITH SOME COMMANDS AND STUFF?

WELL . . . I GOT A LITTLE TIME FREE. MAYBE WE COULD TRY A FEW THINGS.

THREE THINGS TO REMEMBER: BE CLEAR, BE PATIENT, AND NO DOGGY TREATS. A DOG GETS USED TO A LITTLE SOMETHING FOR DOING SOMETHING, AND HE'LL DO NOTHING WHEN YOU GOT NOTHING.

NOW, GET BOUNCER'S LEASH AND LET'S GET STARTED.

OKAY, LET'S START WITH SITTING. GET THE DOG ON YOUR LEFT, GIVE HIM THE COMMAND, AND PULL UP ON THE LEASH A LITTLE. USE A GOOD STRONG VOICE.

BOUNCER! SIT RIGHT DOWN HERE NOW.

KEEP IT SIMPLE AND GIVE HIM A HINT.

SIT!

GOOD DOG!

DON'T FORGET THE THREE Ps: PET AND PRAISE FOR PERFORMANCE.

IT WAS PRETTY CLEAR BOUNCER *AND* ME WERE IN TRAINING HERE, AND LANFORD WAS OUR COMMANDING OFFICER. WE PRACTICED OVER AND OVER.

SIT!

GOOD DOG, BOUNCER. GOOD DOG.

GET DOWN!

KOON

WE RARELY SAW CHARLIE. SHEBA WAS OUR EYES AND EARS.

DID SHEBA EVER GET HURT?

I PROTECTED MY DOG, JUST LIKE ALL US GRUNTS LOOKED OUT FOR EACH OTHER. WHEN YOU'RE IN THE BUSH TOGETHER, YOU'RE BROTHERS.

SO ARE YOUR BUDDIES HOME, TOO?

I DON'T KNOW.

WEREN'T THEY YOUR FRIENDS?

MOST GUYS JUST WENT BY TAGS, LIKE ACE OR ZERO OR FAZ—I DIDN'T EVEN KNOW THEIR LAST NAMES. GRUNTS CAME AND WENT ALL THE TIME, FLY IN, SERVE FOR A YEAR, FLY OUT. HOPEFULLY NOT IN A BODY BAG. ME AND SHEBA MOVED AROUND, WHEREVER WE WERE ASSIGNED.

WHOEVER YOU WERE ON PATROL WITH, YOU HAD THEIR BACK AND THEY HAD YOURS. YOU'D EAT, SLEEP, FIGHT, SWEAT, BLEED TOGETHER—BUT YOU DIDN'T REALLY WANT TO GET TOO TIGHT WITH ANYBODY, BECAUSE NEXT THING YOU KNOW, THEY'RE GONE. TIME'S UP . . . ONE WAY OR ANOTHER.

WHAT ABOUT HADO?

WHAT ABOUT HADO? YOU KNOW, KID, YOU ASK A LOT OF QUESTIONS.

I JUST WANT TO KNOW THINGS . . . MAN THINGS.

WELL, THEN, ASK YOUR DADDY.

I DON'T HAVE ONE.

HE'S DEAD OR SOMETHING?

YEAH. LIKE YOU SAY: "IT DON'T MATTER."

THAT'S 'NAM TALK. NOTHING CAN MATTER THERE, OR ELSE YOU'D START BAWLIN' SO HARD YOU'D LOSE EVERY DROP OF ALL THAT WATER YOU HUMPED.

BUT THIS IS THE WORLD . . . WHERE THINGS MATTER.

YOU WANNA SEE A PICTURE OF ACE?

OKAY.

HADO HAD A BUDDY BACK HOME ALWAYS MAILED HIM PACKS OF KOOL-AID. MIX A LITTLE OF THAT UP IN YOUR CANTEEN AND IT SURE HELPED THE C RATIONS SLIDE DOWN.

WHILE WE ATE THAT CRAP, ME AND HADO ALWAYS TALKED ABOUT "THE MEAL," THE ONE WE EACH WERE GONNA CHOW DOWN OUR FIRST NIGHT HOME. MAN, WE GOT CRAZY TALKING ABOUT FOOD! WE HAD BANQUETS GOING ON! BUT WE ALWAYS ENDED UP AT THE SAME PLACE: A TALL, FROSTY ROOT BEER FLOAT WITH THREE SCOOPS OF THE COLDEST VANILLA ICE CREAM FOR DESSERT.

I CHECKED SHEBA, MADE SURE SHE WAS SETTLING DOWN FOR THE NIGHT. THEN WE CLEANED OUR GUNS. GUYS TALKED ALL KINDS OF NONSENSE, BUT ME AND HADO *FOCUSED.*

WE WERE PLANNING A BUSINESS TOGETHER, A SIGN-PAINTING BUSINESS. I LIKE TO DRAW AND HADO HAD AN UNCLE WITH A PAINT FACTORY. WE EVEN HAD A SLOGAN: *H3L WE'LL SPELL IT OUT FOR YOU.*

H3L *We'll spell it out for you!*

YEAH, WE WERE GOING TO BE *RICH,* ONCE WE MADE IT BACK TO THE WORLD.

SOME NIGHTS, WE JUST LAY BACK AND WATCHED THE FLARES AND TRACERS EXPLODING SOMEWHERE OFF IN THE DISTANCE. ALL THOSE BRIGHT RED, GREEN, BLUE STREAKS, BEAUTIFUL. LIKE THE FOURTH OF JULY, IF YOU DIDN'T THINK ABOUT WHAT THEY MEANT.

AFTER THAT, YOU SPREAD YOUR PONCHO, SCOOCHED IN, AND IT WAS TIME FOR EYELID INSPECTION. YOU'D SLEEP FOR A COUPLE OF HOURS TILL IT WAS YOUR TURN TO WATCH. SHEBA WAS A BIG HELP WITH GUARD DUTY. WHEN SHE WAS AWAKE, I COULD CATCH A FEW EXTRA WINKS.

NEXT DAY YOU'D GET UP AND START WALKING ALL OVER AGAIN.

WHERE WERE YOU GOING?

I DIDN'T REALLY WANT TO KNOW, BUT I COULDN'T HELP MYSELF.

YOU EVER . . . UHH . . . SEEN ANYBODY . . . KILLED?

I'M TELLING YOU A WAR STORY, BOY— AS IN *WAR*, NOT JUST *STORY*.

GOOD THING BOUNCER WAS STILL BOUNCING AROUND IN BETWEEN US. OTHERWISE I THINK LANFORD WOULD HAVE STORMED INSIDE.

ALWAYS SEEMED LIKE WHAT I WANTED TO KNOW SO BAD, HE WANTED TO *UNKNOW*.

I HANDED LANFORD BACK HIS SKETCHBOOK AND DECIDED I OUGHT TO SHARE SOMETHING SPECIAL WITH HIM, TOO, KIND OF EVEN THINGS OUT A BIT . . . *AND* GET ME OUT OF THIS TROUBLESOME CONVERSATION.

HEY, LANFORD. WANNA SEE A COOL PLACE? ME AND BOUNCER LIKE TO GO THERE. YOU KNOW, WHEN WE NEED TO BE BY OURSELVES.

I COULD TAKE A LOOK. THIS DOG NEEDS SOME RUNNING AROUND ANYHOW.

I SHOWED LANFORD A SHORTCUT TO THE FIELD OUT BACK.

BOUNCER STARTED RUNNING CIRCLES AROUND ME WHEN I PICKED UP AN OLD WOODEN SPOON.

I TOSSED IT.

GOOD DOG! LANFORD, DID YOU SEE THAT?

LANFORD?

GOOD CATCH, GIRL. . . .

UH, BOUNCER.

I WAS HUNGRY AND I FIGURED BOUNCER MUST BE, TOO. PLUS, MAMA WOULD BE HOME FROM THE DINER SOON.

I SHOULD PROBABLY BE GETTING BACK.

YEAH, LET'S GO. COME ON, BOUNCER.

SO YOU COME FROM AROUND HERE? IS THIS PLACE YOUR HOME?

YOU GOING REPORTER ON ME?

NO, NO, I . . . JUST WONDERING . . . YOU KNOW, JUST TALKING . . .

TALKING, YEAH. CONVERSATION. I GOTTA GET USED TO THAT AGAIN.

NO, I'M NOT FROM AROUND HERE. I'M JUST STOPPING.

ACTUALLY, MY CAR STOPPED—RAN RIGHT OUT OF GAS. I SAW THE RENTAL SIGN AND PULLED IN.

I WAS REALLY CURIOUS NOW. BUT I WAS LEARNING: GO SLOW ON THE QUESTIONS.

I JUST KEPT QUIET.

IN BOOT CAMP, THEY TEACH YOU NOT EVEN TO *THINK* ABOUT THE VIETNAMESE. DON'T CALL 'EM BY THEIR NAMES, DON'T GIVE 'EM NO RESPECT, TREAT 'EM ALL LIKE VC. AND VC AIN'T HUMAN. JUST DO WHAT YOU GOTTA DO, HERE'S YOUR GEAR.

THEN YOU COME HOME FROM 'NAM, THE MILITARY SAYS "GOOD-BYE, GOOD LUCK, ENJOY YOUR FAMILY, P.S. IT'S A GOOD IDEA NOT TO TELL ANYONE WHERE YOU JUST CAME FROM."

IN THIRTY-SIX HOURS, I WENT FROM DAU TIENG TO DOWNTOWN SAN FRANCISCO.

I GOT THAT ROOT BEER FLOAT. IT WAS GOOD AND COLD—JUST LIKE THE STARES I WAS GETTING FROM SOME PEOPLE.

BABY KILLER!

HERO? HUH!

I SKIPPED SIGHTSEEING AND WENT HOME TO TRENTON.

ALL THE FAMILY CAME AROUND AND SUDDENLY I DIDN'T HAVE NOTHING TO SAY.

BUT IT DIDN'T MATTER: THEY ALL DID PLENTY OF TALKING.

WHILE I WAS GONE, EVERYBODY KEPT ON LIVING; 365 DAYS THEY WERE COOKING DINNER, WASHING THE CAR, CASHING THEIR PAYCHECKS, GOING OUT AND HAVING A LITTLE FUN. NOW THAT I WAS SAFE AT HOME, IT WAS LIKE THE WAR WASN'T GOING ON ANYMORE FOR THEM.

MY OLD PALS TOOK ME OUT TO PARTIES, BUT I JUST DIDN'T CARE. I'D END UP PLAYING WITH A DOG AND THINKING ABOUT SHEBA.

ONE MORNING I WAS AT A DINER.

MY OLD BOSS COMES IN. ALL PUFFED UP AND IMPORTANT-LIKE, HE SAYS LOUDLY, "THIS HERO'S BREAKFAST IS ON ME. TELL US ABOUT HOW WE'RE KICKING BUTT OVER THERE IN VIETNAM, SON."

THAT WAS IT. I LEFT THAT AFTERNOON. JUST GOT IN MY CAR AND DROVE.

WERE YOU KICKING BUTT OVER THERE, LANFORD?

WHO KNOWS? THERE ARE NO RULES. IT'S ALL DINKY DAU. CRAZY. FOR US GRUNTS, WINNING WAS KEEPING YOUR BUTT IN ONE PIECE TILL YOU BOARDED THAT FREEDOM BIRD BACK TO THE WORLD.

IT'S NOT LIKE YOU'RE GIVEN A GOAL OR A GAME PLAN OR SOMETHING. IT'S NOT LIKE THERE'S A BATTLE PLAN AND YOU MARCH OUT, MEET THE ENEMY, AND BOOM! FIRE! VICTORY!

'NAM WASN'T LIKE THAT. THERE WAS NO BIG PICTURE, JUST A LOT OF FUZZY SNAPSHOTS.

I'M TURNING IN.

ALL OUR TALKING MUST HAVE BEEN TOO MUCH FOR LANFORD. THE NEXT DAY, HE WAS STRETCHED OUT IN HIS LAWN CHAIR WITH A HAT PULLED LOW OVER HIS DARK SUNGLASSES. I COULDN'T TELL IF HE WAS AWAKE OR WHAT. I SCUFFED AROUND AND WHISTLED FOR BOUNCER. LANFORD DIDN'T STIR.

COME ON, BOUNCER. LET'S GO FOR A WALK.

BOUNCER TOOK THE LEAD AND HEADED BACK TO OUR FAVORITE SPOT. WE WANDERED AROUND FOR A WHILE. THE PLACE DIDN'T SEEM SO SPECIAL TODAY; EVEN BOUNCER WAS BORED.

SKFFF
SNFFF

BOUNCER, HEEL! *HEEL!* COME BACK! COME BACK!

HELP! LANFORD! HELP!!!

181

THE END.

AUTHOR'S NOTE

"War dogs have served the nation well." — General Colin L. Powell

Whenever people go to war, so do their best friends. Military forces from the ancient Roman army to the Navy SEAL 6 team that carried out the Osama bin Laden mission in Pakistan brought trained dogs along with them. War dogs have worn spiked armor in antiquity and chain mail in the Middle Ages and armored plates during the Renaissance; in modern times, they've been outfitted with everything from gas masks and goggles to bulletproof camouflage vests with infrared and night-vision cameras to give their handlers the dogs' eye view.

Countless soldiers in countless wars kept dogs as mascots or adopted strays in battle-torn areas. Who knows what good luck these mutts brought their masters in combat? But military working dogs (MWDs) are specially trained to support a war effort; they are canine soldiers — and good ones.

Dogs' superior senses of smell and hearing, their capacity to be trained, and their responsiveness to human beings, especially their handlers, make them ideal for many dangerous wartime jobs. Before mass communication was easy, messenger dogs carried urgent information from one military unit to another, often traveling through or around enemy lines. War dogs carry supplies, ammunition, and medicine. They cross battlefields to alert medics to wounded soldiers who need help. They serve as scout dogs, ahead of the infantry, ever vigilant of the presence of enemy patrols or snipers. They can spot machine gun nests and sniff out bombs, mines, and booby traps. They can flush out enemies from caves or underground tunnels. And, of course, war dogs are the perfect guards, keeping military camps or foxholes safe.

European and American military dog trainers prefer certain breeds, such as German shepherds, Belgian Malinois, Airedales, Doberman pinschers, malamutes, and Labrador retrievers. How military dogs are used depends upon the technology and geography of the war.

World War I raged from 1914 to 1918. It was set off by the assassination of an Austro-Hungarian archduke in Sarajevo, Bosnia and Herzegovina, but that was just the match to the fire. Territorial, political, and military rivalries were already simmering, particularly between Germany and Great Britain, which each wanted to be the world's foremost naval power. More than ten million soldiers and civilians died in World War I, which spread across Europe, the Middle East, and some parts of Africa and Asia. The Central powers, which included Germany, Austria-Hungary, and the Ottoman Empire, fought the Allied powers, which included France, Britain, Russia, Italy, and the United States. And dogs were there: carrying messages, pulling supply carts, killing trench rats, and working as mercy dogs, that is, leading medics to wounded soldiers. Germany deployed about 30,000 war dogs, while 20,000 canines joined the British and French troops. Many of World War I's most famous — and most deadly — battles took place in the trenches on the Western Front, which was the site of an unofficial Christmas truce in 1914.

The world was again engulfed in war from 1939 to 1945. And again, the causes were complicated: There had been a great global economic depression; empires had fallen apart because of World War I; Germany was ordered to pay for war damages and its military forces were restricted to a certain size. Enter Adolf Hitler and the Nazi party. Hitler invaded Poland and the die was cast. Allied forces, including Great Britain, the Soviet Union, France, China, and the United States, fought the Axis powers of Germany, Japan, and Italy. More than 100 million military personnel were called up during World War II, not counting dogs . . . that would have added another million to the ranks (though heavily on the Axis side).

When the United States entered World War II, due to the Japanese attack on Pearl Harbor, there were already American rescue dog teams working in Arctic regions such as Greenland, an essential location for aircraft being ferried over from North America to the Allies. Sled dog teams there saved at least 100 aircrew members over the course of the war.

In the summer of 1942, the U.S. war dog program, called K-9 Corps, put dogs and handlers through basic training; some of those dogs were "civilians," volunteered by their owners. By 1944, U.S. Army war dogs had shipped out for European and Pacific battle zones, where they worked as scouts and sentries. The Marines also had war dog units, and their canines, often Dobermans, saw active duty in the Pacific Islands, meaning these "devil dogs" saw combat. Nearly 10,000 dogs served in the U.S. Army, Navy, Marine Corps, and Coast Guard during World War II. When the war ended, many of these dogs were demobilized. They were retrained, given honorable discharges, and went home with their handlers, back to their original owners, or were given to new owners.

The Vietnam War was fought between the Communist north and the anti-Communist south, both of which wanted to control the entire country and each of which had the aid of world superpowers. U.S. involvement in this conflict (on behalf of South Vietnam) lasted from 1959 to 1975, which took the lives of more than 58,000 American servicemen and servicewomen, and became one of the most complicated and divisive chapters in American history. And waging the war itself was just as complicated.

The Vietnam War was fought in hot, dense tropical jungles and rugged mountains, through rivers, rice paddies, and swamps. The enemy was often unseen and moved around mostly at night. War dogs were essential, and nearly 5,000 of them served in Vietnam in all branches of the military. Sentry dogs guarded bases and supply depots. Scout dogs alerted soldiers to snipers and other ambushes when they went out on patrol. Tracker dogs helped locate injured soldiers or downed pilots. Mine and tunnel dogs helped flush out the enemy or signal booby traps. Despite the fact that war dogs were credited with saving thousands of lives in the Vietnam War, most of them never came home. They were classified as equipment and left behind in Vietnam.

Military dogs continue to be a part of the American armed forces and of homeland security. K-9 Corps are deployed in the United States, at military bases abroad, and in the wars in Iraq and Afghanistan. There are about 2,700 dogs of war on active duty right now — helping thousands more human soldiers make it through their active duties.

Semper fido!

FURTHER READING

BOOKS

Barnett, Correlli. *The Great War.* London: Penguin, 2000.

Burnam, John C. *A Soldier's Best Friend: Scout Dogs and Their Handlers in the Vietnam War.* New York: Carroll & Graf, 2003.

Caputo, Philip. *10,000 Days of Thunder: A History of the Vietnam War.* New York: Atheneum, 2005.

Clarke, William F. *Over There with O'Ryan's Roughnecks: Reminiscences of a Private 1st Class Who Served in the 27th U.S. Division with the British Forces in Belgium and France.* Seattle: Superior Publishing, 1968.

Dean, Charles L. *Soldiers and Sled Dogs: A History of Military Dog Mushing.* Lincoln, NE: University of Nebraska Press, 2004.

Ebert, James R. *A Life in a Year: The American Infantryman in Vietnam, 1965–1972.* New York: Presidio Press, 1993.

Edelman, Bernard, ed. *Dear America: Letters Home from Vietnam.* New York: W. W. Norton, 1985.

English, June A. and Thomas D. Jones. *Scholastic Encyclopedia of the United States at War.* New York: Scholastic, 1998.

Greene, Bob. *Homecoming: When the Soldiers Returned from Vietnam.* New York: G. P. Putnam's Sons, 1989.

Hamer, Blythe. *Dogs at War: True Stories of Canine Courage under Fire.* London: Carlton, 2001.

Josephy, Alvin M., Jr., ed. *The American Heritage History of World War I.* New York: American Heritage, 1964.

Lifton, Robert Jay. *Home from the War: Vietnam Veterans; Neither Victims Nor Executioners.* New York: Simon & Schuster, 1973.

Longley, Kyle. *Grunts: The American Combat Soldier in Vietnam.* Armonk, NY: M. E. Sharpe, 2008.

Putney, William W. *Always Faithful: A Memoir of the Marine Dogs of WWII.* New York: Free Press, 2001.

Santoli, Al. *Everything We Had: An Oral History of the Vietnam War by Thirty-three American Soldiers Who Fought It.* New York: Random House, 1981.

Sheffield, G. D. *The Pictorial History of World War I.* New York: W. H. Smith, 1987.

Wallace, Terry. *Bloods: An Oral History of the Vietnam War by Black Veterans.* New York: Random House, 1984.

Weiner, Tom, ed. *Voices of War: Stories of Service from the Home Front and the Front Lines. Vol 1, The Library of Congress Veterans History Project.* Washington, DC: National Geographic, 2004.

Weintraub, Stanley. *Silent Night: The Story of the World War I Christmas Truce.* New York: Free Press, 2001.

DVDS

Ayres, Lew. *All Quiet on the Western Front*, DVD. Directed by Lewis Milestone. Universal City, CA: Universal Studios, 2007.

Berenger, John, Ellen Burstyn, and J. Kenneth Campbell. *Dear America, Letters Home from Vietnam*, DVD. Directed by Bill Couturié. New York: HBO Home Video, 2005.

Choosing Sides: I Remember Vietnam, DVD. Directed by Michael Moriarity. New York: History Channel, 2005.

Douglas, Kirk. *Paths of Glory*, DVD. Directed by Stanley Kubrick. Los Angeles: MGM/UA, 1999.

Font, Louis. *Sir! No Sir! The Suppressed Story of the GI Movement to End the War in Vietnam*, DVD. Directed by David Zeiger. New York: Docurama, 2006.

Kruger, Diane, and Benno Fürmann. *Joyeux Noel*, DVD. Directed by Christian Carion. Culver City, CA: Sony Pictures, 2006.

Lyman, Will. *Vietnam: A Television History*, DVD. Arlington, VA: Public Broadcasting System, 2004.

Meredith, Burgess. *Vietnam's Unseen War: Pictures from the Other Side*, DVD. Washington, DC: National Geographic Video, 2002.

Nguyen, Xuan Ngoc. *Regret to Inform*, DVD. Directed by Barbara Sonneborn. New York: Docurama, 2000.

Vietnam: Homecoming, DVD. Directed by Sammy Jackson. New York: History Channel, 2007.

WEBSITES

American Folklife Center. "Veterans History Project." Library of Congress. http://www.loc.gov/vets.

 "First World War: A Multimedia History of World War One." Michael Duffy. http://www.firstworldwar.com.

"Military Working Dog Teams National Monument." John Burnam Monument Foundation. http://www.jbmf.us.

United States War Dogs Association. "The United States War Dogs Association." Ron Aiello. http://www.uswardogs.org.

SHEILA KEENAN

is an established author of fiction and nonfiction, including *As the Crow Flies*; *Greetings from the 50 States*; *Animals in the House: A History of Pets and People*; *O, Say Can You See? America's Symbols, Landmarks, and Inspiring Words*; and *Gods, Goddesses, and Monsters: A Book of World Mythology*. She is currently collaborating with her husband, artist Kevin Duggan, on a picture book about whales. She lives in New York City.

NATHAN FOX

is an illustrator and storyteller whose work has appeared in *The New York Times*, the *New Yorker*, *Rolling Stone*, *Wired*, and *Entertainment Weekly*, among many other publications. His work has also been published by DC, Vertigo, Dark Horse Comics, and Marvel. He lives with his family in New York City.